**W9-BYY-589**

DISCARD

This book belongs to:

_____

_____

_____

First US edition 2020

Library of Congress Catalog Card Number pending
ISBN 978-1-5362-1564-9

20 21 22 23 24 25 APS 10 9 8 7 6 5 4 3 2 1

Printed in Humen, Dongguan, China

This book was typeset in Lucy Cousins.
The illustrations were done in gouache.

Candlewick Press
99 Dover Street
Somerville, Massachusetts 02144

www.candlewick.com

Maisy's Chinese New Year

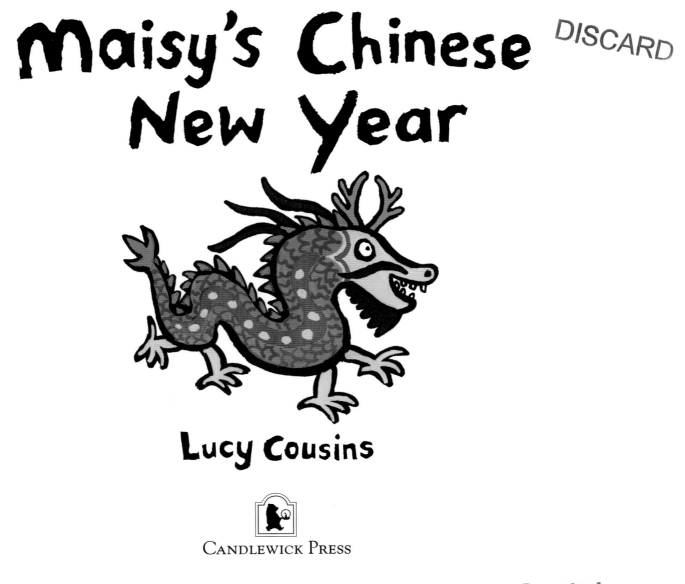

Lucy Cousins

CANDLEWICK PRESS

Tomorrow is Chinese New Year.
Maisy sweeps and tidies
the house to get it ready!

Then Maisy visits a market to buy food, decorations, and a new red outfit.

Red is a lucky color.
What red things can you see?

At home, Maisy waits for her guests.

Who's that knocking at the door?

It's Tiger! She has come
to celebrate. Hooray!

Tallulah, Charley, and Cyril arrive next.
"Welcome, Tiger!" they all say.

Tiger has brought lots of presents
to wish everyone happiness and luck.

They all sit at the table
to eat a delicious feast.
There are so many
things to try!

After dinner, Ostrich
and Penguin come to visit!
They give everyone lucky red
packets with money inside.

"Thank you!" says Maisy.

Maisy and her friends sit to listen to Tiger tell an exciting Chinese New Year story.

"A long, long time ago, twelve animals raced across a great river," she begins.

"The rat won the race, but we celebrate every animal in turn.

dog

pig

rooster

monkey

goat

horse

rat

ox

tiger

rabbit

dragon

snake

And this makes up the twelve-year Chinese zodiac," Tiger explains.

At midnight, fireworks light up the sky to welcome the new year!

Oooh!

Aaaah!

The next day, Maisy takes part in a spectacular parade with loud music and dancing.

Finally, Maisy leads her friends in a special dragon dance for good luck.

sweet rice
cakes

lantern

dumplings

mandarins

blossoms

bamboo

red packet